A Love Beyond Labels:

The Epic Journey to Find His Valentine

Edwin Ross

Copyright © by Edwin Ross 2022. All rights reserved.
Before this document is duplicated or reproduced in any manner, the publisher's consent must be gained. Therefore, the contents within can neither be stored electronically, transferred, nor kept in a database. Neither in Part nor full can the document be copied, scanned, faxed, or retained without approval from the publisher or creator.

CONTENTS

CHAPTER ONE

The Meeting

Jason was a young handsome gay man living in a small town in the Midwest. He had always known that he was different, but he had never really felt comfortable talking about it with anyone. He had kept his sexuality hidden from his family and friends, and he had never even considered dating anyone.

One night, he surprisingly went to a local gay bar. This was off his limits because of his religious background, but he hoped to meet someone who could understand him.

It was a place full of people just like him, and he felt a sense of belonging. He immediately noticed a handsome man sitting at the bar. His name was Ryan, and he was a gay man in the closet just like him. He had just relocated to the neighborhood.

Ryan noticed Jason staring and moved towards him, sitting close to him. Jason developed cold feet but decided to be bold.

Jason was the first to break the ice, saying, “So, I guess we should start getting to know each other, huh?”

Ryan nodded, a little relieved that the conversation had started. "Yeah, let's start with the basics," he responded, smiling at Jason. What’s your name?”

Jason laughed and told Ryan his name. He asked Ryan his name and they proceeded to talk about their interests and hobbies. Jason was intimidated by Ryan at first, but the more they talked, the more Jason felt a connection.
Jason was interested to find out that Ryan liked to read and write, while Ryan was surprised to learn that Jason was an artist.

They talked about their experiences as gay men in the closet and shared their dreams for the future. Jason felt like he could be himself around Ryan, and he felt more confident and freer than ever before.
They talked for hours, getting to know each other, sharing stories, and laughing. As the night went by, Ryan felt like he had known Jason for years despite the short time they had

been talking. He was sure that this was the start of something special.
Ryan couldn't believe Jason was real because he was all he ever thought and prayed for, but he didn't want to feel he was moving too fast to ask Jason out on a date.
Jason in his mind was just fantasizing about all he wants to do with Ryan, in his head they were already done with their first date, married with adopted kids, and having steamy sex.

Jason wished Ryan will just pull him closer and kiss him, but he doesn't know what is running through Ryan's mind. He was afraid of being called desperate or a cheap slut if he should out any of his thoughts to Ryan.

Ryan complimented his looks and dress sense and Jason was blushing all through their conversation saying nothing other than “Yeah” and “Uhunn” or “Hmm” with his eyes fixed on Ryan all night.

So, when Jason was about to take his leave, Ryan made him feel cool and safe with him. Ryan saw him off the bar, and they exchanged contacts.

CHAPTER TWO

First Date

Jason and Ryan were both in their late 20s, and eager to experience their first date. They had been friends for a few days, but the attraction had grown quickly and both were eager to take their relationship to a new level. It was a Saturday night and Jason had taken the initiative to plan the date. He had chosen a local restaurant that was known to have excellent food and a cozy atmosphere. Jason had made a reservation and was already waiting for Ryan when he arrived. Jason was excited to see Ryan, but he was also nervous.

What would they talk about? Would they have a good time? His mind was racing.
When Ryan arrived, Jason was struck by the fact that he had dressed up nicely for the occasion. His hair was well combed back, and he was rocking a nice suit.

Jason felt a surge of happiness that Ryan had put in the effort to look his best.
The two sat down and Jason ordered a bottle of wine. They made small talk as they enjoyed the appetizers and sipped the wine. As the conversation progressed, they began to open up about their lives and shared stories of their experiences. Soon, they were laughing and having a great time.

The main course arrived and the conversation continued. By the time they were done eating, they had talked about everything from their families to their hopes and dreams.

When the dinner was over, Ryan and Jason decided to take a walk. The night was warm and the stars were out. They held hands as they walked and talked about their future together.

Jason felt a connection that he had never felt before. He knew then and there that he wanted to be with Ryan.

When they reached a park, they stopped and sat down on a bench. Ryan took a deep breath and looked into Jason's eyes. He leaned in and kissed him, and Jason responded with the same intensity. The kiss was sweet and passionate, and Jason felt his heart swell with joy.

When the kiss ended, Ryan pulled back and looked into Jason's eyes. He smiled and said, "I think I love you."
"I think I love you too", Jason replied with a smile.
They embraced and kissed again, and Jason felt like his heart was going to burst with happiness. The night wasn't ending soon as they became more inseparable, holding hands like they were glued to each other walking down the road. But Jason had to go home.

After walking a few miles, they decided to go back to Jason's place. Jason was nervous, but he was also excited. This was the first time he was going to be intimate with another man, and he wasn't sure what to expect.

But with all the thoughts running through his head and the fear to disappoint Ryan, he begged for them to take more time to know more about each other before taking further steps.

Ryan turned to him not sure of what to say, smirking at Jason. They both hugged and said their goodbyes.

CHAPTER THREE

Falling in Love

Jason and Ryan had their first date just a few days ago. It was an evening that neither of them would ever forget. They talked for hours and had a wonderful time together. The conversation had been so effortless and natural, it felt like they had known each other for years. When they parted ways that night, both were already feeling something special, and neither wanted the night to end. As they hugged goodbye, Jason knew he was already falling head over heels in love with Ryan.

When Jason woke up the next morning, he couldn't help but replay the memories of the night before. He couldn't stop thinking about Ryan and how he had felt when they were together. The kiss kept replaying in his mind and he seemed to want more of Ryan and regretted not letting him come home with him that night. He had never felt this way before and it was a wonderful feeling.

He realized he had fallen deeply in love with Ryan. He wanted to be with him all the time and he wanted to do anything he could to make him happy. He wanted to show him how much he loved him and that he wanted to be with him forever.

From that moment onward, Jason was devoted to Ryan. He was willing to do anything for him, no matter how much it cost or how difficult it may be. He was always willing to put his own needs aside to make sure that Ryan was happy. He wanted to make sure that Ryan knew that he was truly in love with him and that he would do anything to make him happy. He showered him with gifts and compliments and was always available to listen to him when he needed to talk.

Jason was always willing to go out of his way to make sure that Ryan was happy. He was always ready to sacrifice his own time and energy to make sure that Ryan was taken care of. He wanted to make sure that Ryan knew how much he was loved and appreciated.
In return, Ryan also felt deeply in love with Jason. He was touched by his commitment and devotion and was always willing to do anything

for him. He loved spending time with Jason and was always willing to make time for him, no matter how busy his schedule was.
The love that Jason and Ryan had for each other was deep and true. They both knew that they had found something special in each other and that they would never let it go. They had found a love that was unique and special, something that neither of them had ever experienced before.

They were both so in love with each other that it was almost impossible for them to be apart. Whenever they were together, it felt like nothing else mattered. They were content just being in each other's presence and being able to share the love that they had for each other.

Jason and Ryan's love for each other was undeniable and it was clear that they were meant to be together. They both knew that they had found something special and they weren't willing to let it go.
From the moment they had their first date, they were already deeply in love with each other and they were going to stay that way forever.

Ryan sent Jason a gift on the month anniversary of their first date. It was a beautiful necklace with a heart-shaped pendant that had an inscription that said: "Forever and Always". It was a reminder of their love for each other and it was a symbol of the commitment that they had made to each other that night.

Jason and Ryan had found something in each other that was so special and unique. They had found something that neither of them had ever felt before and it was a love that was so strong and deep. It was a love that was based on trust, respect, and devotion and it was something that neither of them ever wanted to let go of.

As their love for each other continued to grow, Jason and Ryan did not doubt that they were meant to be together. They had found something so special in each other that they knew they would never let go.

CHAPTER FOUR

Keeping the Relationship Secret

Jason and Ryan had been together for a year now since they met and they decided to keep their relationship a secret from their families and friends. They both felt that coming out would be too risky, and they wanted to protect each other from potential ridicule or judgment.

At first, they only saw each other in private and kept their relationship a secret. Jason and Ryan had to be careful not to let anyone know that they were seeing each other. They had to make sure not to display any obvious signs of

affection in public during the day, and they visited each other at home, they had to appear to be straight.
When Jason's family go on trips, he had to stay back because of Ryan. They had the whole house to themselves and did whatever they liked. This was more of a chance for both of them to be more intimate and have more sex or run around the house naked.

The couple also had to be creative in how they exchanged messages. Instead of texting each other simply, they used code words and phrases to communicate with each other. They used aliases when they emailed each other and created separate social media accounts to follow each other's lives. They even had to be careful when they went out in public together, taking

separate cars and entering different doors to avoid being seen together.
Keeping their relationship private had its challenges. Both Jason and Ryan had friends and family who were curious about their relationship, and Jason had to be careful not to slip up and reveal too much information.
He also had to be careful not to make too many references to Ryan when talking to his family and friends.

As their relationship progressed, Jason and Ryan faced more obstacles. Jason's family was very religious and had strong opinions on homosexuality. He was afraid to tell them about Ryan and was worried about how they would react. He also worried that if they found out, they would try to break them up.

Ryan's family was more accepting, but they didn't know that he was dating Jason. He was afraid to tell them, as he was worried that his parents would be disappointed in him. Ryan was also concerned about how his friends would react to him being in a same-sex relationship.

Despite the challenges, Jason and Ryan continued to keep their relationship a secret. They both wanted to protect each other from potential judgment and ridicule. They also wanted to protect themselves from the potential consequences of coming out.
However, as time went on, the couple realized that keeping their relationship a secret was becoming more difficult.

They both wanted to be open and honest about their relationship, but they were afraid of the potential repercussions. Eventually, they decided that it was time to come out and be open about their relationship.

CHAPTER FIVE

Coming Out

Jason and Ryan after secretly seeing each other for over a year finally decided to come out to their families. After much contemplation and many conversations, they had reached a point where they were both ready to share their relationship with the world and their families. They both knew that it would be a difficult process, but they also knew that it would be worth the effort in the end.

For Jason and Ryan, the decision to come out was a difficult one. They had both grown up in conservative households and coming out as gay was not something either of them had considered until recently. They had both gone through years of internal struggle before finally accepting their sexuality and deciding to open up about it to the people closest to them.

When Jason and Ryan finally decided to come out, they both had very different reactions. Ryan was nervous and scared, but he was also excited to finally be open about his relationship with Jason. He knew it would be difficult, but he was also looking forward to the sense of freedom and acceptance that would come with it. Jason, on the other hand, was more apprehensive. He was worried about the potential backlash from his family and how his parents would react.

He was also scared about the possibility of being rejected by his family and the wider community. Despite his fears, Jason was determined to follow through with the decision to come out of the closet.

When the day came for Jason and Ryan to tell their families, they both experienced a mixture of emotions. Ryan was relieved to finally be able to be open about his relationship with Jason, but he was also scared about how his family would react. Jason, however, was more focused on the potential reactions from his parents and how they would respond.

Once Jason and Ryan had told their families about their relationship, the reactions were mixed. Some of their family members were supportive and accepting, while others were less understanding. Those who were more open to the idea of a gay relationship offered their love and support to Jason and Ryan.

Those who were less accepting struggled to understand the concept of a gay relationship and why it was important to Jason and Ryan. Despite the mixed reactions, Jason and Ryan were both relieved to finally be open about their relationship. They also felt a sense of freedom knowing that they could be open and honest about who they were without fear of judgment.

They were both proud of themselves for coming out and for taking the first step in being open and honest about their relationship. Coming out to their families was a difficult but important step for Jason and Ryan. It was a process that took courage and strength, but it was also one that ultimately helped them both to be more comfortable in their skin and to be more confident in their relationship.

They both were relieved to have finally come out to their families and to be able to be open and honest about who they are.

CHAPTER SIX

Valentine's Day

Jason and Ryan had been together now for a year and some months but they already felt like they had been together forever. It was a day that Ryan and Jason had been looking forward to for quite some time – their first Valentine's Day 2022. They wanted to celebrate that day together publicly as openly gay men. It was the perfect opportunity to show each other how much they meant to each other. The night before, Jason decided to have a sleepover at Ryan's.

It was early in the morning on valentine's day when Ryan awoke, feeling excited and nervous at the same time. He looked over at Jason and smiled.

He couldn't believe that his dream had come true - he was in a relationship with the man of his dreams. He was determined to make this the best valentine's day ever.

After getting ready for the day, Ryan and Jason set out to get breakfast at a local cafe. They both ordered the same thing - a large cappuccino and a croissant. As they ate, they talked about their plans for the day. Ryan had been planning something special, but he wanted to keep it a surprise.

When they finished breakfast, Ryan took Jason's hand and led him to a nearby park. They sat down on a bench and watched as the sun rose and the day gradually came to life. It was a beautiful morning, and they couldn't help but feel grateful to be here in this moment together. The next stop was the botanical gardens, which were in full bloom. They strolled around, admiring the vibrant colors and fragrances of the flowers. Ryan had also arranged for a private tour guide, who took them to some of the more hidden parts of the garden. It was a special treat for the two of them, and they appreciated the time alone together.

After the tour, they had lunch at a restaurant near the garden. Ryan had made a reservation for the two of them and had chosen a romantic corner table for their meal. They had a delicious meal, and Jason couldn't help but feel special - Ryan had gone out of his way to make it a perfect day.

After lunch, they decided to take a walk along the beach. The sky was a breathtaking array of colors as the sun set. They stopped to watch the waves roll in and out, and they talked about their future together.

It was a perfect moment, and they both knew that it was the start of something beautiful. They spent the rest of the evening back at Ryan's place, where they watched a romantic movie and cuddled up on the couch. Ryan had made dinner for the two of them, and it was a lovely way to end the perfect day.

When it was time for bed, Ryan and Jason held each other close, grateful for the moment they were sharing. They had spent their first valentine's day together as openly gay men, and it had been perfect. They both knew that this was just the start of something wonderful.

CHAPTER SEVEN

The Vow

Jason and Ryan had been together for two years now and it was time for them to celebrate their anniversary. They had been through a lot in those three years and it was a time to reflect on all the good times they had experienced together.

It was a beautiful night. The stars were shining bright in the clear sky, and the air was filled with love and happiness. Jason and Ryan were sitting on a bench in the park, looking out over the city skyline. They were talking about everything they had been through, the highs and lows, and how much they had grown together.

As they talked, Ryan reached into his pocket and took out a small box. He unwrapped it and brought out a charming ring. He then reached for Jason's hand and said, "Jason, I love you more than anything in the world and I want to spend the rest of my life with you.

Will you marry me?"

Jason was overwhelmed with emotion and tears welled up in his eyes. He leaned forward and kissed Ryan gently on the lips.

"Yes," he said, "I will marry you."

They hugged each other tightly and Ryan put the ring on Jason's finger. They were both filled with joy and excitement. They had come a long way in their relationship and now they were ready to take the next step.

This was a huge milestone for them both and a symbol of their commitment to each other. They continued to celebrate their special day, visiting all the places that held special memories for them. They stopped for dinner at their favorite restaurant and then went to the movies.

The next day, they decided to have a wedding celebration. They invited all their friends and family to join them in celebrating their union. Jason and Ryan exchanged their vows and their kiss sealed their commitment to each other. Everyone was in tears, happy for the couple but also in awe of their courage and strength. They had overcome so much in the past three years and now they were ready to start their lives together as a married couple.

The wedding celebration lasted until late in the night and Jason and Ryan were exhausted by the time they got home. They had a lot of planning to do for their future and they were both looking forward to a long and happy life together.

Jason and Ryan had come a long way since they first met. They had faced a lot of challenges and had overcome so much together. Now they were ready to embark on a new journey as married couple.
The next morning, Jason and Ryan woke up and looked into each other's eyes. They were filled with love, hope, and determination for the future. They were ready to face the world together and to continue to celebrate their love for each other.

CHAPTER EIGHT
Growing Old Together

It had been 7 years since Jason and Ryan had gotten married. After their wedding, the two decided to adopt kids and buy a house. It was a big decision for the couple, but one that they both agreed would be the best for their growing family.

At the start, it was a challenge for Jason and Ryan to find an affordable house that met their needs. The couple had to search through many listings, and eventually found a house that was within their budget. It was a three-bedroom

home with enough space for their kids and all the furniture they had purchased.
Once they had the house, Jason and Ryan began to focus on the adoption process. They had to go through all the paperwork and interviews, but eventually, they were approved and their home was filled with the laughter and joy of their adopted children.

The couple was now faced with the task of raising the kids and teaching them the values and beliefs that they wanted them to have.
Jason and Ryan both had their ideas on how to accomplish this, but they agreed on the basics: respect, honesty, and hard work. They also wanted to teach their kids to be kind and charitable and to always think of others before themselves.

As the years passed, Jason and Ryan watched their kids grow and develop into young adults. They were proud of their children and the lives they had created for themselves.

With the family growing, the couple decided to make some changes to the house. They added rooms, updated the appliances, and even began to garden in the backyard.
The years were filled with laughter and joy as Jason and Ryan grew old together. They watched their children graduate from college and pursue their careers. They celebrated their children's marriages and welcomed their grandchildren into the world.

For Jason and Ryan, the journey of growing old together had been filled with love and hard work. It was a journey that had taken them from a single couple to a loving family. They had worked hard to build the life they wanted, and now they felt a sense of pride and satisfaction in all that they had accomplished.

As the years passed, the couple found themselves surrounded by their children and grandchildren. They celebrated holidays together, shared stories of their youth, and watched their kids and grandkids grow up. Even though they were growing older, they were still just two people in love, and they were proud of all they had accomplished.

Jason and Ryan, growing old together would always be remembered. The couple had found a way to make their dreams come true and they were happy that they had embraced the challenge of building a family. They had shown their kids the importance of love and hard work, and they were grateful that their journey had been filled with so much joy.

www.ingramcontent.com/pod-product-compliance
Lightning Source LLC
LaVergne TN
LVHW020529160826
845677LV00015B/3980

* 9 7 9 8 3 7 2 0 7 3 7 8 4 *